THE GOOSE THAT LAID THE GOLDEN EGGS

Reading Consultant: Prue Goodwin, Lecturer in literacy and children's books

ORCHARD BOOKS
338 Euston Road, London NW1 3BH
Orchard Books Australia
Level 17/207 Kent Street, Sydney, NSW 2000

First published in 2011
First paperback publication in 2012

ISBN 978 1 40830 965 0 (hardback)
ISBN 978 1 40830 973 5 (paperback)

Text © Lou Kuenzler 2011
Illustrations © Jill Newton 2011

A CIP catalogue record for this book is available
from the British Library.

1 3 5 7 9 10 8 6 4 2 (hardback)
1 3 5 7 9 10 8 6 4 2 (paperback)

Printed in Great Britain

Orchard Books is a division of Hachette Children's Books,
an Hachette UK company.
www.hachette.co.uk

B53 003 576 3

AESOP'S AWESOME RHYMES

THE GOOSE THAT LAID THE GOLDEN EGGS

Written by **Lou Kuenzler**
Illustrated by **Jill Newton**

ORCHARD

Old Aesop lived long, long ago
(he was an Ancient Greek, you know).
The many fables that he spun
are always wise and often fun.

These rules will keep you fit and well
and others will not SHARE your smell!

This Aesop tale is strange and funny.
A farming couple longed for money.
They longed for coins, they longed for cash
they longed for jewels that they could stash

So when their goose laid eggs of gold,
you should've seen their joy unfold.

(Before we start – a little word:
do NOT get too fond of the bird!
Things DON'T turn out very well
for the goose who laid a golden shell.)

We've rushed ahead, which is a shame.
We need to start before Goose came . . .

The farmer lived a simple life
in a pokey cottage with his wife.

They had no plasma screen TV,
no games console or huge PC.

They had no lights, electric power,
indoor loo or walk-in shower.

They washed themselves in a shallow
  ditch.
It's no surprise they longed to be rich!

Each week they saved a little cash
to give the lottery a bash.
"A million pounds would change our life,"
said the hopeful farmer's wife.

The farmer said, "My dear, that's true!
We'd buy FIVE THOUSAND geese,
brand new!"

But Mrs F had other plans –
she smiled and squeezed his muddy hand.

They hoped their numbers would come up
but, sadly, they were not in luck.
It was a dream – a bit of fun . . .
Alas, their ticket *never* won!

One day they went out to a fair
and entered for a raffle there.
Imagine Farmer's great surprise
at winning Goosy as a prize!

She was the pride and joy of Farmer
who didn't (yet) have plans to harm her.
He hoped that she'd lay eggs to eat.
A lovely early morning treat!

Come wintertime, he *might* just skin her . . .
she'd make a cracking Christmas dinner!

Next day he took a cup of tea,
and went to see what eggs there'd be.

He bent down low – he had to stoop –
to fit inside the poultry coop.
The goose was in the box of hay
he'd made for her so she would lay.

"How many eggs for me, my dear?"
he said, and peered beneath her rear.

We had a goose — perhaps your cousin —
who always laid us half a dozen.

He lifted up her feathery bum –
and saw that she had laid . . . just one.

"That's no good!" He sounded stern.

Goose, you're going to have to learn to lay a bigger clutch than this!

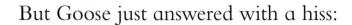
But Goose just answered with a hiss:

I think you'll find that **ONE** is fine!
Just step outside and see it shine.
You silly fool! That egg you hold
is made of solid carat gold!

Amazed to hear the goose could speak,
the farmer went to take a peek.
He took the egg into the light
and saw that it was shining bright.

He knew at once the gold was real . . .
and gave his wife the egg to feel.
She quickly felt the heavy weight
and knew that they could celebrate.

The more a piece of fine gold weighs,
the more it means the merchant pays!
We'll never need to scrimp and beg,
we're set for life with this nest-egg!

"Then buy some chickens!" Farmer
  whooped.
Off they went, without a word.
They never even thanked the bird.

Goose flapped her wings, "I wouldn't
  mind.
But I've got such a sore behind."

A normal egg pops out with ease.
A big gold whopper takes more squeeze!
You need strong muscles, bum and legs
to lay enormous golden eggs.

The gold egg fetched a handsome price.

We're rich enough to buy things twice!
Two pairs red shoes, two pairs black,
two with no toes, two with no backs.
Two pairs of boots, two pairs of clogs,
some ballet pumps, trainers – for jogs . . .

The farmer also longed to spend –
he treated himself to pretty hens.

A cockerel, pigeons, a fine peacock,
a budgerigar and a cuckoo clock!

Next day, before the new cock crowed,
they searched the coop for eggs that
glowed.
They found one sitting in the hay.
So once again they shopped all day!

I have a list of things to buy . . .

Then hurry, darling. So have I!

A dove for him, stilettos for her,
a partridge chick, red boots with fur.
It very soon became absurd –
for ever buying shoes and birds.

Each new morning Goose would lay.
Always the same – one egg a day.
The couple grumbled, wanting more:
"She should lay three – or even four!"

"Patience!" said Goose, "You're
   getting greedy!
Laying eggs is never speedy.
Six minutes each for solid gold
and four for silver, so I'm told.
I can't just fire eggs out my bum.
The most I'll lay each day is ONE!"

The farmer's wife had another plan.
"If Goose can't get them out – we can!"
She took her husband to one side
to tell him what they should decide:

Listen, I'm not being funny,
there must be eggs inside her tummy.
Each day she gives us next to nothing
yet Goosey there has golden stuffing!
Let's slit her open! I can't wait
for piles of gold upon our plate!

The farmer thought it should be tried:

He grabbed the Christmas carving knife.
"I'll stick it in!" he told his wife.

Although I pity poor old Goose,
we have to set our money loose!

Goose cried, "I know just what is up.
You fools think gold's inside my gut!"
She flapped her wings and tried to fly,
but knew her time had come to die.
"Just wait a moment! Drop the knife!"
she begged the farmer and his wife.

But Farmer charged – the murdering
  thief –
and slit the goose from underneath.

Poor Goosey gave a deathly shiver.
"Inside me there's just guts and liver.
No precious gold, I'm sad to say.
The most you'll find is goose pâté."

But – such a shame – poor Goose was
  dead.
Her empty guts spilled out and bled.
(You were warned, right from the start,
not to take Goosey to your heart.
It's still a grim and grisly end
for our poor and generous feathered
  friend.

Perhaps in heaven Goosy sings
and flies around on golden wings!)

The silly farmer and his wife
cried, "We were fools to take her life!
Because of our atrocious greed
we've killed the very thing we need."

Without the goose alive to lay
there would be no more eggs each day.
"Because we hoped for more inside,
we're left with nowt!" the farmer sighed.

The birds he'd bought flew off that night.
(They'd seen the goose and taken fright.)

His wife's new shoes were soon worn
 down
and there'd be no more trips to town.

The couple once again were poor.
No fun for those two any more!
There was no money left for treats,
like fancy fowl and well-shod feet.
They had to struggle through again
with muddy wellies and no hen.

It seemed a cruel and rotten joke
they'd once had golden shell and yolk.
The moral learned is tough, hard-boiled:
with too much greed things just get
  spoiled!
Take good care of what you own.
Don't be greedy – never moan!

Written by **Lou Kuenzler**
Illustrated by **Jill Newton**

All priced at £8.99

Orchard Books are available
from all good bookshops, or can
be ordered from our website,
www.orchardbooks.co.uk,
or telephone 01235 827702,
or fax 01235 827703.